Beyond Death

Leanne Halyburton

Contents

The story of a boy who forgot to look both ways...

Part 1

It didn't hurt. He felt exhilarated, free, as if he was flying. He thought about all the people he loved and a great wave of gratitude and affection swept over him - and then he realised that something was different. The car that had come from nowhere and tossed him through the air like a crash-test dummy. The screams of those who looked on with horror; broken glass, the flowing warmth of blood, the sound of crying…

He was dead. That was it. One minute a teenage boy larking about, charging across the road to catch up with his mate, the next he was crunching and smashing his way across the bonnet of a swerving car before being launched like a limp but deadly missile into the tarmac. But, he felt okay. In fact, he felt better than okay; he felt strangely relieved, as if a weight he had been unaware of had been lifted from his shoulders. Except that, he didn't have shoulders. He knew where they should be, could kind of feel them, but they weren't there. It was like being an amputee.

1

He had read that people who have had a limb removed continued to feel sensation such as pain or itching, in a leg or arm that no longer existed.

And then he felt guilty. What about his mum? She'd go mad, it would really screw things up for her. She'd had enough to deal with without him getting himself killed. And what about Scanna, his best friend? Who'd he hang out with now? Maybe he should go back… if he *could* go back, that is. He didn't want to, though - he felt really happy, and 'alive' somehow… he just didn't want other people to be sad.

"Don't worry - they'll be alright! It's life… love and loss are just part of the experience. There *will* be emotional pain for them to deal with, but they'll keep going. That's what human souls do."

What? Who *said* that? Maybe nobody said it… maybe it was just his own mind talking. It sounded kind of right though, and he wanted to believe it - *whoever* said it.

"Daniel Jackson was a bright, popular boy. He was always cheerful, always polite, and he was a credit to the

2

school. We are all in a state of shock and he will be very sadly missed." Mr Allan, head of St John's High, exhausted, the permanent bags under his eyes having reached a whole new level of sagginess.

Anne Jackson, grey faced and heavily sedated, lying on the bed, staring sightlessly at the ceiling.

Jade Jackson, slumped on the floor, leaning against her bed, knees pressed into her chest… a sodden tissue clutched tightly in a wet fist, gasping for breath in between uncontrollable sobs for a lost big brother.

Flowers, teddy bears, football shirts, piling up on the pavement outside St John's High. Even people who couldn't stand Daniel Jackson, and those who acted as if he didn't exist when he was alive, came and left their offerings - which Daniel thought was bloody funny. But, he couldn't be angry… he just couldn't seem to feel it, and things that used to bother him didn't seem to matter so much anymore. Only love, and concern for certain people.

He understood, too, that there were 'processes' for him to go through: at first, there is the feeling of lightness and freedom, though from what, he wasn't sure.

Then there was realisation - and then there was choice. He just knew that he was free to choose, that nothing was going to be forced upon him, and that there was no timescale to honour. He didn't really understand it, but he *knew* it. He thought all of his dead relatives should have appeared in a bubble of light by now, but that hadn't happened. He didn't feel as if he was alone, though… which, weirdly, wasn't scary.

For now, he just wanted to *be*, to think, and to feel the essence of his mother, his family, his friends. He was aware of them in his mind, as if they were close. He knew what they were thinking and feeling, and he experienced tenderness and concern - but not sadness, not fear, not loneliness. He just *knew* stuff. He knew that everyone who was grieving for him would be following him, one way or another, at some point in time. He knew that life mattered, but in terms of existence it was way shorter than… non-life? He knew that there were way more dead people than living people, and he knew that being 'dead' felt more alive than being alive, which was odd. Or, at least it should have been odd… but it made perfect sense.

"You okay?"

Whoa, who *is* that? He jumped, as if someone had leapt out from behind a door, taking him by surprise.

"It's me - don't you remember?"

"Bloody hell... Kev Mitchell! You died in a car crash last year, didn't you? Didn't expect to see you."

"Two years ago, actually. Thought I'd come and show me face."

Silence, and then Daniel suddenly 'got' the joke. Kev didn't have a face, just like he didn't have shoulders. And yet, he recognised him. Plus, Kev's face had been pretty much obliterated when he'd gone through the windscreen and head first into a tree. Still funny though, and Daniel was genuinely pleased to 'see' him.

"I thought I was supposed to meet all my dead relatives, and that they'd come and take me to where they live... but the only person who has shown up is you."

"Sorry to disappoint you, mate - you're stuck with me as a welcoming party, for now at least. You'll get to be with all of the people you want to, when you're ready."

Daniel thought that he *was* ready, and then realised it would have freaked him out if a load of old people, most of whom he'd never met in his life, suddenly arrived and carted him off somewhere. He wouldn't have known who to ask for if he'd had the chance - probably his Grandad Bill. He definitely wouldn't have thought of asking for Kev Mitchell… but it was still cool talking to him, though.

"*Why*? What did he ever do to anyone? He was 15 years old, my baby! Why *him*, when there are paedophiles, terrorists, and murderers, still walking this planet? If there *was* a God, why would he let this happen? Why take my child away from me? It should have been *me*, not him. Why, why, why?"

Anne Jackson, screaming out questions for which there were no answers. No answers that would be acceptable. No explanation that could, or would, ever be adequate enough. And no-one would ever be insensitive - or brave - enough to try and pacify, using mumbled words that would only burrow like sharpened bullets into an already broken heart and mind.

"She's really upset! Isn't there *any* way I can let her know that I'm okay?"

"Not at the moment Dan, sorry mate. You should have seen *my* mam. She was really peed off. Gave her another excuse to pour more booze down her neck for the next 6 months."

Kev was strange, Daniel decided. What he said and what he meant were not the same. He just knew that Kev loved his mum...

"'Course I love the stupid cow, but she was, and still is, a bleedin' nightmare."

"How did you know… ?" Daniel started but didn't need to finish. We are *thinking* words, not speaking them, he concluded. I will have to be careful what I am saying… er, no, *thinking*, I mean - in future.

"You'll get the hang of it. You're still in transition. How do you feel now?"

"What's transition? I feel… actually, I feel heavy. I felt light before. Now my arms hurt, and so does my head. But, I haven't actually got arms and a head. What's going on? What does it mean?"

Feeling weak, heavy, a little afraid now, and glad not to be alone… with the sudden warmth of Kev somehow wrapping itself around him - embarrassing, and yet nice, like a comforting hug.

"You are making the transition from one level of awareness to another. From one dimension of existence to another. What hurts the body hurts the spirit and vice versa.

The bruising on your soul is coming out, mate, but you'll be alright. If you don't fight it, if you just let it happen, you'll be fine."

"Okay… right… I mean... I feel *really* tired, I want to go to sleep… I don't know what to do...."

"Just let go and drift off, Dan. You have to dream now..."

Part 2

He is a little boy, five years old, dressed in blue shorts and a green and brown striped polo shirt. On his feet are the black and brown trainers he loved, and ankle socks. There is a gentle breeze lifting the ends of his dark brown fringe, and the sun is warming his arms.

"Dan-Dan, little man!"

He hears the familiar call, but for a second is confused... and then he sees the man walking towards him, coming more and more into view as he climbs the hill upon which Daniel realises he is standing.

"Grandad! Grandad!"

A great gulp of pleasure and emotion fills the throat of the hurtling child as he propels himself into the arms of the stocky, grey-haired man.

"Now then! What the hell are you doing here so soon, young man?"

Grandad Bill, Anne Jackson's father. Died at the age of 67 after suffering a heart attack, when Daniel was only eight.

"I don't know. It seems a long time ago now… I was older… I don't know."

Still hugging the hips of the older man, breathing in his familiar scent, a mix of oil, the outdoors, and toast. Daniel had forgotten that smell - had forgotten how much he'd missed the gruff voice, the strong arms, the solid sense of masculinity. Grandad Bill knows everything. He is funny but he can be tough, as well. He doesn't like tantrums, "stupid baby behaviour", he says. He doesn't like bad manners at the table, or wasted food. He thinks kids should play out and learn how to do stuff with their hands. He gets cross when Grandma Brenda fusses around and panders to the children, so she is sneaky with the treats, and when slipping a plate of barely touched food away from the table.

Grandma Brenda! He'd almost forgotten about her, and a wave of guilt hits him in the heart.

"Don't worry about her, she's never far away," Grandad Bill chuckles, doing that mind-reading stuff that seemed to be so popular around here. And then Daniel sees her, coming up the hill, soft, sagging, rosy cheeks, grey-white hair worn short, leaning forward as she walks, causing her ample bottom to stick out.

"Well, well, well, fancy seeing you here! Come and get a Grandma cuddle."

Her body feels warm and squashy, and smells of sweet almond and chips. She was never herself after Bill died, and developed all kinds of health problems. She got pneumonia and died, when Daniel was ten.

"I didn't want this for you, it's too soon." She squeezes him tightly, pressing her face into the top of his head, and he knows she is holding back the tears. "But, it's lovely to see you, anyway."

"It's his time," Grandad Bill responds in a no-nonsense tone. "It's his destiny. I don't know why you keep questioning that. You've been here long enough to understand how it works."

"Oh shut up, know-it-all." She winks at Daniel. "Look at him, barely born and then he dies. I still don't think it's right."

Daniel suddenly understands. He doesn't know how but he does. Bill and Brenda have love for each other and there is a mutual sense of unspoken connection, but they aren't together. Not together in the sense that the living mean, anyway. He had heard people talking when someone died, saying that now they would be together with this or that person, or that they'd be looked after by other dead relatives… but it isn't exactly like that. Bill had said 'Don't worry about her, she's never far away,' and he remembered his mum saying that she could feel Grandma Brenda's presence, loads of times, and it had freaked him out. Brenda lives for her family, they are the centre of her world, she has always been happy living the same life, doing the same things, day in and day out. Until Bill died, and then she kind of lost interest. Grandad Bill is different. He loves his family, and a great sense of duty and responsibility has always kept him living the same kind of everyday life, doing what needs to be done. But, he has always been more of a free spirit than Brenda, and would love to travel, to explore, and he died with many unrealised dreams and desires within him. His heart got tired of the yearning, and threw in the towel, as they say. Brenda, dependent upon routine and sameness, and always more connected to the past than the future, struggled to go on without Bill, even though she still had her family. In death, they are both free from the limitations of physical life, are free to be who they are. Being spiritual really only means being true to the real self, not all that stuff living people like to *think* it means. Of course, with that comes the need for common sense, and respect for others - it doesn't mean that we can just do what we want to, regardless. In death, Brenda sticks close to the family and the dimension of the living. Bill keeps in touch in his own way, but is busy being the spirit he truly is, deep down inside.

Daniel, in his five year old form, is aware of these two people he has known and loved, and now understands them in a deeper, more meaningful way - a way that he never *would* have, when alive… even if he had lived to be a hundred and one. And suddenly, he sees them change; Bill becomes a handsome young man with a square jaw, a strong, direct gaze and a good head of dark brown hair. He carries himself proudly, with confidence, and there is an air of anticipation, expectation and hope about him.

Brenda is slim, pretty, with soft chestnut hair tied back. She has blue eyes, clear skin, and her hand rests upon her abdomen. She yearns to have a baby, to create a family, to surround herself with familiarity and safety. That has always been her dream. Together, she and Bill made that dream come true, but she never really understood Bill's restlessness, and so she ignored it. They did okay though, and made it through to the end… and now she understands. Bill still has some exploring to do. Together, but apart.

Part 3

"This one's a bit of an angry sod, he doesn't want to play ball at all."

Daniel is back with Kev. He isn't five anymore, and Grandad Bill and Grandma Brenda have gone… but yet he can still feel them. It's like he's had one of those dreams that are so real they stay with you for days - completely different to ordinary dreams - about random weird stuff that never makes sense.

"Enjoy your visit?" Kev interrupts his pondering, and it is clear that he is smiling, pleased to have shown Daniel something important, something he doesn't yet fully understand. Without waiting for an answer, he continues.

"This guy doesn't like what he is experiencing. It's not what he expected."

Daniel was suddenly aware that the atmosphere had changed. He shivered, as if a big dark cloud had drifted across the sun, blocking out the light and the warmth.

"Who is he? And what's it got to do with us?" He wanted to remove himself from the pervading sense of misery, frustration, and oppression, hanging heavy in the air, but Kev seemed unfazed.

"He's just caused mayhem - shot three people and got himself blown out of life, courtesy of several bullets to the head and chest. He thought he was going to be welcomed as a hero and is pretty peed off, trying to avoid going through a life review."

Jesus! Scary stuff. "What's a life review?"

"Well, in what is less than a split second, he'll experience everything that others have experienced as a result of association with *him*. Good and bad. It's not a judgement from an outside source - it's an independent, in-depth look at his own motivation, intentions, and actions, throughout his life. Only *he* can make his mind up about what his life really meant and was worth, overall. You've got to feel a bit sorry for him, it's not a great experience for someone who has lived the kind of life he has."

"He was a dick, by the sound of it.'" Daniel didn't agree with Kev's point of view. "And how come I didn't have a what-do-you-call-it… a life review?"

"Because, my hapless friend, you are young and haven't had enough life experience, in *this* life at least, and you haven't had enough time to accumulate a comprehensive history worth scrutinizing. So, count yourself lucky."

"Oh. So what about you, did you have one?"

"Being a bit older than you, and being a bit cocky, yes I did. But nothing like this guy's - this is really gritty stuff. Not all bad though. He wasn't a maniac 24 hours a day, *every* day of his life. He did love some people and they loved him. And, he did plenty of productive things, mainly *before* he allowed his mind to become screwed up."

"So what will happen to him now?"

Daniel had heard about Heaven and Hell, never given any serious thought to either, but maybe he should do now… or was it too late?

"Depends upon himself. He can become stuck in a nightmare of his own making and convince himself that he is trapped, with no way out. Or, he can choose to face up to and accept the impact his choices and actions had on *other* members of the human race, and also the collective energy of life on Earth - and then he could begin the healing process. Could go either way."

"Well there's no competition, is there? Why would he choose the first option? That doesn't make any sense."

"God knows, but they often do. It's obviously too hard for them to let go of old beliefs, and to face up to their own cock-ups".

There was way too much stuff to take in. A zillion questions battled for prime position in Daniel's mind... did he even *have* a mind, or maybe he was *only* a mind now. Another bloody question to add to the collection. He decided he'd start with Kev. What's really going on with him, what's *he* about? He waited for him to jump in with some smart-arsed response, but there was silence.

"Okay Kev, how come you know all of this stuff? You're like some kind of oracle, not an idiot who was always messing about doing things he shouldn't be doing - driving like a maniac in a car he shouldn't have been driving in the first place. And, what is all this about dreams? I was a kid with my grandparents, and then I wasn't. And you said the angry guy - who I can't actually *see*, by the way, even though I can feel a *really* bad mood hanging around - could choose to become stuck in a nightmare. It was great when I first died. It was great when I was with my Grandad and Grandma, but it's getting a bit weird now, and I don't like it."

Silence... and then laughter. Kev was laughing at him, taking the mickey. Daniel bristled with indignation and hurt feelings, and would have gone off in a huff if he'd known how to. But then, the warmth of the Kev hug he'd felt earlier returned, and he realized that the laughter wasn't aimed at him, but was because of him.

"Sorry Dan! You are young, or at least you were when you died, and you are *different*. You have potential, and you are having a bit of a crash course at the moment, no pun intended. Me, I had a good think when I died, and I decided I didn't want to waste death. I would have wasted life, and that's a dead cert. I was never stupid, even if I behaved as if I was. But, I cut my own life experience short. You're kind of like me, only better. You would have been an idiot sometimes, had you lived, but you would have been a pretty decent human being, overall. However, you'd have gotten caught up with everyday life and wasted your biggest talents: imagination, instinct, intuition, and creative thinking. You can choose to use them now - for the sake of the cause."

Daniel felt blown away, but something within him stirred, something he kind of recognised but couldn't quite bring forward.

"That's an Irish band, isn't it? What have they got to do with all of this?"

"That's the Corrs, you daft sod! The cause isn't an official title, but it's what I call it. You know how they say the universe is expanding? Well, the universe is only a tiny part of a much bigger field of existence, and it is that bigger field that is actually evolving and growing. The universe has to grow with it, and human energy plays a massive role in the whole process."

"Okay, I can kind of get my head around some of that, I think, but it doesn't explain what the cause is."

"Movement against resistance, mate. There is an ongoing battle in the dimension that is known as life on Earth, a battle between light and dark, over forward and backward movement. The cause is all about getting people, dead and alive, to wake up and think about stuff, to be part of the uplift and forward movement, not stagnancy or backslide."

Daniel was stumped. Most people - no, *all* of the people - he knew would have thought Kev was off his rocker if he'd gone around spouting this stuff when he was alive. Kev himself would have thought he was off his rocker, never mind anyone else. But yet, it touched something within him, something kind of familiar… again, the thing he couldn't quite pin down.

"Okay, so this guy, the shooter, what's he all about?"

"He's all about the backward slide, a player in the quest to prevent positive growth. It's his way or no way - or so he thinks. In reality, he has, sadly, been recruited by the dark side, a pawn in a much bigger game. A big man behind a gun, but a pawn nevertheless. He now gets to choose his own fate. Dying could be the best or the worst thing that ever happened to him. Depends how connected he can feel to the real cause, and not the one that led him to get his head splattered over an impressively large area."

"Is this actually real? I thought that dead people just, well, went off and lived with all of their relatives somewhere in the sky, doing sod all for eternity… unless they were really bad, and then they probably get sent somewhere not very nice."

Daniel realized he'd picked this unexplored idea up from his mum, who liked to watch strange people on telly who claimed to be communicating with those who had 'passed', as they called it. She talked about it as if that is how it all is, and he just kind of assumed she knew what she was going on about. He hadn't given it much thought until he himself became one of those who had 'passed'. He suddenly wondered if he'd be on TV at some point, being summoned to send his love and say how wonderful everything is, in the world of 'spirit'. Imagine if he told them about all of this Star Wars kind of stuff that Kev keeps talking about, instead. The thought of it made him laugh… he could just picture the reaction!

Then he remembered the shooter, the dark angry cloud.

"So, why are you involved with this nutter? And why are you involving me? And, did *you* make me come back here instead of letting me stay with my Grandad?"

"Whoa mate, one thing at a time! Look, as I said, I decided not to waste death. I figured that if I could help others to choose not to waste death as well, I'd be doing something productive. I've seen where the bitter, angry spirits go, in their minds, and it is a bloody dark place. And *that* collective energy is not good for the human race, either. So, that's why I am involved. And I elected to be your very own personal tour guide when you bit the dust, because I knew you had a lot of potential others don't have… or at least will never tap into and use. But, it's up to you, you can just enter into your own personal dream state and leave the dirty work to idiots like me, if that is what you really want. And no, I didn't make you come to this place, I don't have any power or control over you - it was your own choice."

Daniel wasn't convinced about the last bit, but he didn't argue. "So, I can choose what I do, who I see, and what I experience?"

"Absolutely. I am only showing you things, explaining something about the big stuff. You can choose to turn away and experience a different reality *right now*, if you want to."

It was tempting to say the least. Daniel suddenly felt tired again, felt the need to sleep, to get away from Kev and the overload of information. Phrases like 'rest in peace' and 'sleep well' are used when people die, but this didn't feel very restful.

"I need to think - I just want to sleep for a while… "

Part 4

He was sitting on a wall, overlooking a beach. Little blue waves, edged with lacy white foam, rolled in, breaking over caramel coloured sand. Crisp white sails of little boats dotted the horizon and small, puffy clouds lay strewn across an almost turquoise sky, like scatter cushions.

A small group of people were busily building a sandcastle, halfway down between the wall and the sea, and the sound of laughter and happy chattering reached him on a brine-scented breeze. One of the group, a man, looked up and waved to him.

"Come on and join in," he called. Grandad Bill.

Daniel pushed himself off the wall, made his way down a few steps that were cut into the rock, and crossed the sand. As he approached the chattering gaggle, a young girl turned her face towards him, smiling. She had his eyes, and although he didn't know her, somehow he knew who she was.

"You're my sister," he stated. "I've never met you but I know you".

She stood and wrapped slim arms around his neck, and hugged him. There was sand on her hands, in her auburn hair, and on her cheek. A smattering of freckles tumbled across the bridge of her nose, and she smelled of sunshine and ice cream.

"I *am*... clever you!" she laughed.

Her eyes sparkled as she gazed intently into his face, scrutinizing every detail.

"We look similar," she concluded. "I'm Emily, by the way. That's the name Mum gave me and the one she uses when she talks to me in her head."

Emily did not make it into the world as such, she died in the womb, six months into Anne Jackson's pregnancy, 18 months before Daniel was born. He knew his mother had lost a baby girl but it wasn't something he had given much thought to. He cringed with embarrassment when he thought about that, but Emily just laughed.

"Don't feel bad, it all happened before you were born. Here..." she handed him a little green spade. "Help us finish this grand sand castle. By the way, this is Thomas, your uncle on dad's side, even though he is younger than you. He died when he was four." She gestured toward a small blond haired boy with a round face and a turned up nose, who grinned at him and gave a little wave. "Hiya."

"And this is Mary," Emily continued. "She used to live next door and helped Mum a lot after Dad left, and she was very fond of you!"

Daniel tried to remember the lady with the tired but kind face, who looked as though she had no teeth, and whose bosom almost reached her tummy. He didn't want to appear rude, but he couldn't really find her in his memory.

"Don't worry son, you were just a babby. I died of lung cancer when you were about three, but I've kept an eye on you ever since."

Daniel murmured his thanks and turned to acknowledge Grandad Bill.

"I'm glad to see you again, I thought maybe I wouldn't."

Bill laughed. "Course you'd see me again, you nitwit. It just takes time, that's all. There's a lot for you to take in."

"I know, tell me about it. I'm not sure about Kev either, he goes on about stuff that seems well over the top."

Bill knew that Daniel was unnerved by what had been revealed to him, and so he kept it light.

"Oh, Kev's alright, he's a smart one," he replied, as he made little windows out of shells and pebbles on the side of the sandcastle. "Just give it all some time, there's no hurry. Oh, by the way, you have an appointment coming up."

"An appointment? Who with and where at?" Sodding hell, Daniel fretted, what wonders have they got in store for me now?

"Your mum is going to visit a medium, she wants to try and get in touch with you."

Daniel's heart leapt, or at least it felt as if it did.

"Really? Wow. That'll be great. Am I going to be on telly?"

Bill laughed. "No, thank goodness! It's a private session. But don't get your hopes too high. These things don't always work out as wished for. It can be a bit hit and miss. Just have an open mind and take it for what it is."

"Okay, I'll try. How did you know anyway?"

"Aha" Bill said, tapping the side of his nose. "I must be psychic."

Daniel laughed. "You've done this before," he stated. "Haven't you?"

"I'm afraid I have," Bill grunted, sticking a seagull feather into the top of the castle. "You've got to show willing."

"How will I know where to go, and how will I know what to do?

"Don't worry, you'll know on both counts. And anyway, you won't be on your own."

"Why, who… ?"

Bill stared at Daniel over the top of his glasses, and pointed a finger toward himself.

"Because, muggins here has been roped in as well."

"Your mother will be here in a moment, she's just parking the car."

Grandad Bill was trying to appear casual, as if he was just waiting for a bus or something… but Daniel could feel the tension, and the older man was standing very close to him.

"Where are we, and who's she?" Daniel whispered. They were gazing into a small room, in which a woman, around the same age as his mum, and with shoulder length brown hair, was seated at a table. There was an empty chair opposite, and the woman seemed to be… waiting. Her hands were resting in her lap, and her eyes were closed. It wasn't totally clear though… Daniel wondered if the room was smokey, because he was struggling to see properly. He *could* see, but it was as if he was looking through a dusty lens, and it was frustrating.

"That's Julia, she's the one your mum has come to see. She's a… oh, here's your mum now."

A man appeared at the door, holding it open for someone who squeezed past him.

The man spoke, but his words didn't register with Daniel.

"*Mum*!" He half yelled and half sobbed, at the same time, and he felt Grandad Bill's presence, a bit like the Kev hug, only better. He couldn't believe what he was seeing. He knew it was his mum… he could feel her, with every inch of his being, but she didn't look the same. She was thinner, paler, and she looked older than he remembered. Even through the haze, he could see that she was a shadow of the woman she used to be. It made him feel so sad… angry even.

"I shouldn't have died! It's my fault."

"Now, now lad, keep it together. You're going to need all of your energy, but it'll be worth it in the end."

The older man had been prepared for this, and he was going to help the boy get through his first 'communication'. It was always the trickiest, especially if the wires got crossed, and the link muddled up.

Julia was speaking. "Hello Anne, please sit down."

The already tearful woman, clutching a packet of tissues, slid into the chair, and took a gulp of air.

"Thank you," she whispered.

"I can see that this is very difficult for you," Julia soothed, "but please don't worry. Obviously you are here because you want to make contact with someone who has passed, and I will do the best I can. Sometimes the link is strong, sometimes it isn't. And, if I don't make immediate contact with the person you are hoping to hear from, it won't be because they aren't available, or don't want to talk with you… it will be because I haven't been able to pick up their frequency. Do you understand?"

Anne Jackson sighed softly, and blinked. "Yes… I do. But I hope… I hope that…"

"I know, I know," the medium reached across and patted her hand. "I will do my best."

Julia closed her eyes, and breathed deeply. Daniel experienced a sudden jolt, as if a flash of lightning ran through him… and the haze started to lift. The room became clearer, and he could see the blue of the walls, the gold of the carpet, the fine grey streaks in his mother's hair… and she was wearing his black and red sweatshirt… the one he'd only worn a couple of times before… well, you know…*before.* It cheered him up, though, and made him feel close to her. He noticed that it still had a little stain on the front, where he'd dropped a tomato sauce covered chip. She'd obviously picked the top up off his bedroom floor, and put it on without washing it. Not like her… normally she'd have had it off his back and straight into the washing machine!

Grandad Bill elbowed Daniel in the ribs, grinning… doing that mind reading thing again. Julia opened her eyes and began to speak.

"I feel the presence of a young man… and my chest and my head hurt…" She winced a little. "Of course he isn't feeling that pain now, it is only a way of identifying him. He is wearing a red top… a sports type top…"

"That's my son!" Anne Jackson gasped. "He… he was hit by a car… and that's his favourite football top you can see him wearing." Her voice was swallowed by a sob, as she pressed a crumpled tissue against her lips.

Daniel looked down at himself; "I'm wearing my footie top? Oh yeah, so I am… nice one!"

"Is he okay… is he with anyone?" Anne asked, voice quivering.

"Well, of course he's fine," Julia murmured. "Let me see. He appears to be with an older man… broad, silvery grey hair, a ruddy face… your father? He had a big pain in his chest, not long before he passed." Bill nudged Daniel again, and winked. "I'm up," he said.

"Yes… yes, that sounds like my dad! Thank goodness… I'm so glad Daniel's not alone!"

"Oh, he'd never be alone," Julia laughed. "And when people die, they are more alive than we are… they are *more* free, because they are operating within a much higher vibrational dimension than this one!"

The medium closed her eyes again, and Daniel felt the shift in energy. He found himself kind of talking… but without words. He thought about his beloved Hugo Boss aftershave… not that he shaved… and lasagne… his absolute fave food… and spending hours in the shower, playing his music, full blast.

Julia touched on all of these. She told Anne she could smell an expensive perfume… a man's perfume. And she could 'taste' Italian food… and she could hear loud music and singing. Maybe she couldn't hear him totally clearly, Daniel thought, but she certainly got the gist of what he was thinking. And Anne recognised everything. Daniel was starting to really get into it, now.

"He's showing me something heart-shaped… it looks like a little pendant… silver coloured…"

Anne nodded. "I put it in the coffin with him. He'd given it to me the Christmas before… before he died. He took my heart with him, so it seemed to be the right thing to do. Can you tell him I love him… we all love him… and we will miss him forever?"

"You just told him yourself!" Julia laughed. "And anyway, he already knew. So, what's this now?"

She closed her eyes again, and appeared to be really concentrating.

"Ah… he's rubbing the top of your head… and he says "See ya later, Annie!"

Anne Jackson actually laughed out loud. "Oh my God! He often did that on his way out of the door! He would pass my chair and ruffle up my hair, because he knew it bugged me, and he'd say, 'See ya later, Annie'… and I would say MOTHER to you, you cheeky little bugger!"

Bill could feel his grandson's relief… *and* his daughter's. Okay, the grief would never leave her until she herself made the transition, but for now she was smiling… for now she believed, wholeheartedly, that her son still existed, and that she would see him again one day. She was reassured that he wasn't lost and alone. Tonight, she would sleep a little better, though the tears would still slip between her flickering eyelids, slide down her cheeks and dampen her pillow, as she dreamed. One step at a time… one day at a time…there was no other way of doing it.

Anne Jackson wiped her eyes, took a deep breath, and sat up straight.

"Thank you, Julia. You have no idea what this means to me. And please, tell my dad and mum that we love and miss them too… and thank them for looking after Daniel.

Part 5

"How did it go? Did you manage to get anything across to your mum?"

Kev seemed to just show up, out of nowhere, but Daniel was pleased. He was still buzzing from the experience, and he was keen to talk about it.

"Yeah… it was weird! I just kind of thought stuff, and this woman… Julia… picked up on it, and told my mum about it. She couldn't hear everything exactly right… apart from the bit about me calling her Annie, and ruffling her hair… but it was pretty close! I think it really cheered my mum up. She was smiling when she left, anyway. I can't wait for next time. Maybe I'll get to see Jade, and Scanna, too."

"All in good time, my little mate… all in good time. So, what are you going to do now?"

Daniel was surprised by the question. He hadn't thought about it… didn't even realise that he could choose.

"I don't know. What else is there to see and do here? Apart from hanging out with nutters. I'll give that a miss, thank you very much."

Kev laughed. "Pussy cat! Scared of the bogie men! Seriously though, don't worry, you'll figure it all out. We travel through dreaming… remember, how you felt as if you wanted to sleep, and then suddenly you were somewhere else?"

"Oh yeah… that's right. But did I *choose* to go where I ended up? I don't remember choosing. I met people I didn't even know… but I KNEW them, if you see what I mean."

"Oh you chose, you just weren't aware! The more you do it, the more aware you become. There are experiences you won't want to have, and some you won't be able to have at this stage in your existence… but, as I said, you'll figure it out. Feeling sleepy yet?" And suddenly, Daniel realised that he was indeed drifting off, and that Kev's 'voice' was fading away into nothingness.

Part 6

"**H**ere, get this down you whilst it's still hot!"

Daniel was sitting at a table, in a warm, cozy kitchen, and Grandma Brenda was placing a steaming bowl of jam roly-poly and custard in front of him. He was himself, as he was, not younger. He gazed down at the sweet-smelling pudding.

"We get to *eat*?" He hadn't eaten a thing since he'd hit the tarmac… hadn't been hungry, or even thought about food. But now his tummy seemed to be rumbling… the non-existent tummy.

"What do you mean? Of course we get to eat! You do come out with some silly things sometimes! Do you want a cup of tea, or milk?"

Daniel stared up at the soft-cheeked woman, drinking in everything about her. He could feel her need to nurture, to organise, to feed others… and suddenly he understood. He was in Brenda's reality now…

"Brenda? Grandma to *you*!" she snapped, with a twinkle in her eye, and Daniel laughed out loud. "Does everyone here have to keep bloody listening in to everything I'm thinking?"

"Language, young man. And yes, they will, until you learn how to communicate properly. It'll come, but in the meantime, think about what you're thinking!"

Grandad Bill was picking plums and dropping them into a basket. He threw one to Daniel, commenting on how sweet and juicy the crop was this year.

This year, Daniel pondered. What IS a year, here? How long had it been since he died? He honestly had no idea. He looked over at Bill, who was standing, hands on hips, gazing down at the basket of purple fruit, lost in his own thoughts. Daniel wondered why the older man wasn't responding to *his* thoughts. He seemed not to be able to hear him… or maybe he was ignoring him.

"Grandad," he thought, rolling the plum around and around in his hand. "Can you hear me?"

Bill turned around, and Daniel could feel his surprise. It was easy to forget that everything here was about feeling. The illusion of having a physical body was a strange one. Everything was about mind… about being conscious, and aware, about responsive energy. And yet, with a sense of having flesh-and-blood-and-bone bodies, that actually can't exist in a non-physical world. Or, maybe that was just his own personal version of reality.

"Of course I can hear you. When you want me to. I don't hear you when you don't want me to."

"So, things are changing, then. You used to be able to hear everything I thought… remember?"

"Ah yes, but now you're getting the hang of things, and you aren't such an open book… and a blessed relief *that* is, I can tell you!"

Daniel laughed. And then a question suddenly arose, like a bubble rising from the bottom of a glass of lemonade.

"How old am I?"

Grandad Bill stared at him, over the top of his glasses. "As old as your tongue and a bit older than your teeth."

Part 7

Daniel was in his bedroom. It wasn't a conscious decision, more of a thought, a memory, that led him there. The door was closed, the curtains drawn, and the room was warm, almost airless. The single bed he'd had since he was five was exactly as he'd left it, the day he… didn't come back. The same duvet cover, striped red, black, and blue, the same pillow case, creased, where his head had left a slight dent in the pillow. One strand of his dark brown hair, caught up in the fabric. A small browny coloured stain on the crumpled bottom sheet, from spilled Coca Cola.

Daniel rubbed his eyes, trying to clear his vision. He could see, but it was as if he was looking through a faint blue mist. He turned to open the curtains, and nothing happened… he reached out, but the material did not respond to his touch, which really bothered him. He felt a wave of anxiety, rising within his… chest area… and a little sick. Here was here, but *not* here!

"Don't panic. Take your time, and try again." Grandad Bill's voice seemed to flow through Daniel, more of a feeling than a sound, and he immediately felt better, though slightly irritated that even here he was obviously *still* thinking out loud!

He 'breathed' deeply, steadied himself, and reached out, slowly, tentatively… and the curtain fluttered, as if caught in a breeze.

"Yes!" Daniel gave an air punch, but then worried that maybe it *was* a breeze that had caused the curtain to ripple. Determined, he focused on his intention and reached out again, sweeping his hand to the left… and the curtain slid backwards along the rail, revealing late afternoon sunlight.

"I can do it, I can *do* it!" Daniel was so relieved he didn't know whether to laugh or cry. Being here without being able to touch anything would be like being… dead.

He became aware of a sound, slight, muffled, and tried to work out where it was coming from. He kind of recognised the sound, but couldn't quite place it. And then, the essence of his mother flooded through him, and he knew that it was her. It was her voice he had been feeling, rather than hearing… and she was close.

And there he was, next to her bed, and she was sleeping, fully clothed, on top of the quilt, lying on her side, softly weeping and murmuring in her sleep.

"It's okay Mum," he whispered, reaching out to touch her hair. "I'm still around."

Anne Jackson gave a little shudder, sighed, and then visibly relaxed. Her lips moved, and Daniel tried to catch her words.

"Love you son."

"I love you too. And Jade. I'll *always* be here…"

"And so will I!"

Daniel jumped. "What the… ?"

"I come and visit her too. Often."

Emily, freckle-faced sister, mischievous in demeanor, was grinning up at him.

"How… when… did you get here?"

Daniel was confused. He wasn't sure whether he was pleased to see her or not. He kind of wanted to be the one to take care of his mum. Emily shrugged. "I felt you, and I knew you were here. Don't be jealous Danny… she misses you more than she misses me."

If it was possible for a deceased person to blush, Daniel's face would have brought the traffic to a halt.

"I'm *not* jealous," he muttered. "I was just thinking that…erm…"

"You were thinking that you want to be the one to look after her. It's okay. She does love and miss me, but she experienced you in her life, she raised you, and you were going to be a part of her future. You were going to get married, and have children. She didn't just lose *you*…she lost a daughter-in-law, and she lost her grandchildren. Of course she lost me, too, but I existed in her mind and heart. She imagined who I would be, and how I would look, and how I would behave. I got to become the perfect child! But you… well, you were part of her 'real' life. You did things like smoking in the park and then using body spray to try and hide the smell! She knew, you know… she was just gathering evidence, and waiting to pounce. Lucky you died when you did, otherwise you'd have gotten a hell of a row! Oh, and she *would* have found out about the cans of cider you drank in Scanna's dad's shed."

Daniel was speech (or thought) less; another shock to the system, another realisation to come to terms with. Bloody great. Emily laughed, and linked her arm through his. She seemed to somehow sparkle, and once again he caught the scent of sunshine and ice cream… she was like a warm breeze on a summer's day.

"Don't be sad, she'll be here herself, one day, when it is her time, and she'll ground you for having gotten yourself run over! Don't think you're off the hook for that one!"

Daniel laughed, and felt a million times better. Yes, she *would* be here, too, one day. He wasn't in a hurry for his...no, *their*...mum to die. He wanted her to have a long and happy life, but there was no two ways about it: everyone dies sooner or later, and so would she.

"Here, I've got a pressie for you!"

Kev was trying to hide a smirk, as he handed a large paper bag to Daniel.

"What is it?" Surprised, Daniel peered into the bag, and saw that it was filled with… white feathers.

"Feathers? What the hell am I supposed to do with these?"

"Oh, I don't know. Chuck 'em around when you go on one of your little visits. The non-deceased love 'em, for some reason! Proves we've been there, apparently." Daniel really didn't know whether Kev was serious or not. He wasn't sure how to react, in case the white feather thing was real, and something he should have known about. He was fed up with coming across as thick, and being laughed at. Which is a pity, because that's exactly what Kev did.

"Ah, sorry mate! Just winding you up! I heard all about your visit with your ma. Pretty impressive, actually. You did well, by all accounts. It's hard going at first, so hats off to you."

"Oh. Thanks. My sister showed up, as well. You know, it's funny, it was as if our mum knew we were there, even though she was asleep. I hope I can go and see her again."

"You will, don't worry. And yes, she did know you were there, but she believes she was dreaming. She will only tell Jade, and her best mate Maureen, about the dream, because she knows they will understand. It is the way it is, I am afraid...more often than not they are scared to believe that a dead loved one has communicated with them, just in case they are being daft. But the 'dream' stays with them, as if it was real, and they don't forget. It's as good as it gets."

Daniel chewed over what Kev had just told him, trying to understand, but feeling more and more sleepy. It had been a long… day? Week? Month? He really couldn't say, which was weird. And then he remembered the feathers.

"So, I'm supposed to leave these behind, am I?"

Kev laughed out loud, pleased that his joke had paid off.

"You daft sod! You can if you want, mate, you can if you want…"

Part 8

The sea was green... no blue... maybe gold. It shimmered and changed colour constantly, and Daniel realised that there was no horizon. There was an ocean, or what appeared to be an ocean, more vast than anything he had ever seen, but no horizon. An endless tide of fluid movement, complete with silvery crested waves... but no horizon. This wasn't the beach he'd visited before. This was like no beach he'd ever seen before, in his life... or in his death.

Struggling to process what he was seeing, Daniel suddenly became aware that grandad Bill was standing on the shoreline, staring out to sea. And beside him was a broad, browny-yellow coloured dog. Daniel experienced a rush of surprise and hopeful joy... could it be... was it possible?

"Tof!" he yelled. "Toffee... is that you?"

The dog's ears pricked, its head swivelled, and joyously barking, it set off towards him. Seconds later, it hurtled into him, furiously licking his face with a hammy pink tongue.

Tears tumbled from Daniel's eyes, and he hugged the big labrador, burying his face in salty-sea fur.

"Tof, you're *here*! I can't believe it… I bloody missed you, you big daft idiot! I was really peed off when you died… I thought I'd never see you again."

"Well, you thought wrong,"Bill said, as he arrived alongside them. "Did you think animals are different to humans? They're all souls too, you know… just in a different shape and form."

"I… I don't know. I hadn't gotten round to thinking about it," Daniel sat back on the sand, rubbing the big dog's head. "But how come I've only just seen him now? Where's he been? I thought he'd really want to see me?"

"One step at a time, I've already told you that," his grandad responded, in a gruff but kindly tone. "There's a lot to take in. Anyway, what do you see out there?" He stared out to sea, and Daniel followed his gaze across the endless colour-changing stretch of ocean.

"Nothing," he said. "I can't see anything. There isn't even a horizon!"

"Course there is!" The older man chuckled. "Can't you see it?"

Daniel felt the old familiar frustration rising up within him, and turned away from the sea, burying his face in Toffee's neck.

"I said I couldn't, didn't I?"

Grandad Bill was silent for a second, and then he patted the boy's head.

"Well, not to worry. Rome wasn't built in a day. Anyway, I'll be going over there soon!"

He sounded excited, but Daniel suddenly felt afraid.

"What do you mean, you're going over there? Where is *there*? And why'd you have to go?"

Bill lowered himself onto the sand, next to his grandson, taking a couple of seconds to make himself comfortable.

"I've earned the right to go," he said firmly. "But I will be coming back, and you can always reach me if you really need to, whilst I'm away. You can help your grandma to look after Toffee here. And there's other stuff for you to do, as well."

Daniel let out a sigh… well, more of a release of pressure… and slumped against a large rock behind him.

"So, what are you going to do there? And how long will you be gone?"

"Oh, I'm going to hang out with one or two souls who have done something worth doing," he chuckled. "Learn a few things I didn't know! And let me ask *you* something, lad. How long have you been here?"

"What… here on this beach? Or since I died?"

"Either or both."

"Well… erm… I think…" Daniel tried really hard to work it out. How long HAD it been since he bounced off that car? How long had he been sitting here, cuddling Toffee? He was trying to pin time down, but it kept slipping away from him, like a bar of soft soap in the bath.

"Exactly!" said Bill, triumphantly. "When you see me again, if you can tell me how long I've been gone, I'll give you a tenner!"

Part 9

There was a tremor… like an earthquake, only it wasn't outside. Daniel felt it, deep within himself, and it wasn't a nice feeling.

"Incoming," Kev said, before Daniel even had a chance to question the sensation.

"Incoming? What's incoming… ?"

Daniel experienced a wave of fear and dread… whatever it was, it couldn't possibly be good.

"Hold it together, mate… there's nothing to worry about… there's a bit of a job to do, that's all."

A second tremor rippled through Daniel, causing him to shudder involuntarily, and what can only be described as a wall of sound descended, engulfing him. He desperately wanted to cover his ears, shield his eyes… empty his mind. But then it was over… silence settled for maybe a second, maybe a minute… Daniel couldn't say… before it was shattered by a piercing, terrified scream.

"Mum! Mum, help me! Where are you?"

Daniel wanted to sink to his knees, to un-hear the soul-wrenching, insanity-inducing cry that cut like a razor blade through soft flesh. It was a female voice, and she sounded young.

"Kev, what's going on?" Daniel tried to locate his friend… he could feel him, but he had become disoriented. There seemed to be movement, emotion, pressure, all around, and he couldn't get his bearings.

"It's okay… keep cool, everything'll be alright."

Daniel felt Kev move swiftly past him, almost through him, and then he saw her… a young, pretty girl of about thirteen, green eyes wide with terror, clutching and tearing at her dark blond hair, mouth open, emitting a now silent scream. Kev grabbed her, pulling her close to him and held her tightly. "It's okay," he whispered. "It's not your time." He touched her eyelids, gently, closing them, and she relaxed into his arms. "It's not your time," he repeated. "Your mum is waiting for you, Lily… you can go back now…"

Bloody hell, Daniel breathed. This was serious shit. He felt like one of those balloons hanging off the ceiling after Christmas, dull, deflated, and wrinkly. But he was also in awe of Kev. The way he handled that girl… that was amazing. It didn't take a genius to work out that she had almost died, but not quite, and that she had to go back. He wouldn't have known what to do. He had a lot to learn.

Kev touched his shoulder. "How're you doing?"

Daniel tried to respond, but nothing would come. And he could feel that Kev was distracted… something else was coming. And then he saw them. A woman, around thirty, tightly holding onto a small child. A man, maybe thirty five, and an elderly woman and man together. A young guy, late teens or early twenties, a woman around the same age as his mother, and a boy of about six. They were quiet and confused but calm. Daniel felt sad for them, but somehow knew that they'd be okay. He realised that he and Kev were not the only ones greeting the 'incoming'. There were a number of souls moving amongst the new arrivals, informing, soothing, and comforting. A female, not young but yet not old, tended to the woman with the child. She leaned over them, hand on the woman's shoulder, and Daniel noticed how her presence calmed them. The woman gazed up at her, genuine relief spreading across her pretty face. The child laughed, and Daniel felt anxiety and tension oozing out of him, like cream from a squashed eclair.

"This is too effing much," he breathed again, and immediately felt the disapproval of an elderly lady tending to the man and woman who had arrived together. "Sorry," he mumbled. And then he saw her. She was about sixteen, slim, with shoulder-length, light brown hair. Dressed in a tee-shirt and shorts, bare legs tanned, she looked as if she had simply been lifted from a beach and dropped into his world. She was fidgeting with her hands, whilst obviously trying to appear unfazed. Daniel approached her nervously, not sure whether or not he should.

"Hi. Erm, are you alright?"

"Yes… I think so. Am I dead?" The girl looked directly into his eyes, and he could sense that she was holding her breath… well, if she actually had breath to hold, that is.

"Yes," he responded, quietly. "You are."

"Which means that you are, too, then. Right?"

"Yes, I am!" He couldn't lie.

"Well, okay, that's not so bad then. I mean, you're young, aren't you? How old are you?"

Daniel had to think… how old *was* he?

"I was fifteen when I died… I'm not sure how old I am now. It's hard to say, here. How old are you?"

"Almost fifteen… in three weeks and two days. I look a bit older than I am, or so I have been told. I didn't expect to die so soon It doesn't make sense, really."

Daniel sat down next to her.

"What happened? Can you remember?"

She stared into space for a second, frowning, as she tried to gather her thoughts.

"There was a festival… it was sunny… there was music, lots of people on the streets...oh…" her face clouded. "There was an explosion. And that's it… that's all I remember." She hugged her knees to her chest, dropping her head so that her shiny hair splayed across her legs. Self-consciously, Daniel patted her shoulder and tried to work out what to say next.

"It's actually okay, being dead," he stammered. "Not what I thought it would be like… not that I actually thought much about it, to be honest, before I… er, died."

The girl stared up at him, from beneath a tangled fringe.

"How'd you die?" She asked.

"Ran in front of a car. Stupid way to die… could have been avoided, if I'd have had half a brain. Not like you… erm, I mean, if you don't mind me saying? Sounds like you had no choice…"

"No. No choice… I don't think. Is it just me?" She looked around, appearing to be coming to terms with the situation. "Ah, no, it isn't just me. And there's a baby… shame."

There was silence for a second or two, and then Daniel remembered his manners.

"Sorry, what's your name? I'm Daniel, and my friend... who is around here somewhere... is Kev."

"Micci. Short for Michelle. So... what happens next?"

Daniel didn't need to respond, much to his relief (he had no idea what was supposed to happen next), because Kev appeared and took over.

"Hello Michelle, it's nice to meet you. It's a bit sudden, I know... but then isn't that always the way? I see Dan here has been keeping you company. Don't be put off by him... not all dead people are such losers!"

Micci glanced from him to Daniel, and then, realising that it was just banter, laughed.

"Okay, so where are all my long-dead relatives? Isn't there supposed to be a welcoming party?"

"That's *exactly* what I said!" Daniel exclaimed. "I thought they'd all be queuing up... I was bloody relieved when they weren't! But you will get to meet your relatives... well, I did anyway. I suppose it's the same for everyone..." he looked to Kev for confirmation.

"We need to get you settled first," Kev responded. "You've got all the time in the world to catch up with the old timers... they aren't going anywhere... yet."

Part 10

Micci had a bit of a dip, when the realisation fully hit home. She grieved for her parents, her dog, her best friend… and the plans she had made for her life. She seemed to fade, somehow, to become colourless… as if she was dying, even whilst dead. To Daniel, it was incredibly alarming… he hadn't seen this before. Kev told him not to worry, she would be taken care of… that there are souls who go into shock, but who are always okay, thanks to the loving care of the healers. They never *become* lost. Lost souls arrive lost, and stay lost, unless they choose a different dream-reality. And that is how Daniel came to be aware of the dimension of lost souls. And that is how his first visit came about… with a lot of persuasion from Kev.

"It's up to you," he said. "You don't have to face these unhappy little buggers if you don't want to, but they do exist, and you'll learn a lot about the human mind, not to mention what souls can put themselves through. I'll be there, you won't be alone."

Daniel remembered the angry guy who'd been shot in the head, and couldn't think of one good reason to hang out with other nutters like him. He couldn't care less what humans put themselves through… that was their choice. But, a part of him was curious. Terrified, but curious. What would it look like, what would it feel like, this dimension of lost souls?

"Is there any chance of getting stuck there, not being able to get out again?"

Kev hesitated, before answering.

"Not if you keep your mind on me. We can't stay too long anyway, otherwise it becomes… er, tricky."

"Tricky? *How* tricky, exactly?"

"Don't worry about that mate, I'll take care of you. Just focus on me, and I'll do the rest."

And there they were, in a place that appeared to be endlessly grey, and all Daniel could see and feel was a heavy, humid, seeping mist. And then, he and Kev moved into an icy cold pocket, and it was as if steel fingers had forced their way into his very being. Daniel stiffened, and mentally held onto Kev even harder than before. A freezing, foul smelling wave of air hit him, as if someone… or something… was breathing in his face, and yet he couldn't see anything other than the mist. And then he heard the voice... whispering, menacing: "you're weak, aren't you? You think you're getting out of here, don't you? I'm going to absorb you, you little bastard, and you'll spend eternity inside of me!"

Daniel let out an involuntary scream, and wished with everything he could muster that he hadn't let Kev talk him into this… and then he heard Kev's voice, strong, solid, firm.

"You can't touch him and you can't reach him, so back off! I'll ask you again, as I have a hundred times already: *are you ready and willing to take the first step out of this hell-hole*? Are you brave enough to move towards the light, face your own demons, and begin the healing process? *Are you*?"

In response, a wild, non-human scream echoed agonisingly around and around inside Daniel's mind, and he was overwhelmingly grateful when he realised that Kev was blocking it.

"So be it," Kev muttered, and they moved on.

Daniel felt icy cold hands ripping at his very core, but the worst thing was the increasing feeling of hopeless, helpless, suffocating depression. It hung heavy in the air, pushing him down, bringing all kinds of horrible thoughts into his mind. He felt as if he was hanging off Kev's back, like a big sack of rotten potatoes, and he wanted to slither to the ground in a stinking puddle of putrid mush. Kev's voice beat its way into his thinking, dragging him out of the devastating trance.

"Fight it! Stay with me!"

Daniel focused every ounce of his concentration on Kev, who was talking to entities that couldn't be seen, warning them off or persuading them to leave their self-imposed hell, to move toward the light. And then, what could only be described as a long, soft sigh filled Daniel's mind, and he heard:

"I'm ready. Please help me."

Kev whooped jubilantly, and Daniel felt as if someone joined them. He was so tired, so heavy, he could barely string his thoughts together, but he knew that another soul was also hanging onto Kev, and he felt sorry for him. Kev, however, seemed as happy as a pig in poo, and shouted, "right, let's get the hell out of here!"

And there they were, out of the dimension of lost souls… Daniel, wheezing, feeling as if he had been swimming for his life in a rancid, green lake, Kev, sweaty and exhausted, and what can only be described as a 'thing', limp and shapeless, the colour of rotten meat, emitting gasping sounds. Kev laughed out loud, punching the air. "Got one!" he yelled.

Daniel stared at the now wriggling creature, struggling to hide his disgust.

"Got what? What *is* it?"

"That my friend, is a lost soul, ready to face himself and begin the healing process! Do you know how hard it is to come back with one of these? Almost frigging impossible!"

Suddenly Daniel understood. Kev had just saved a soul, and he felt like sobbing. How many times had Kev entered into that shithole of death, on his own, to try and save the soul of a human being who had gone astray in the worst way imaginable? Kev was becoming a real hero in Daniel's eyes, despite still being an arsehole at times.

"Why does it look like *that*?" Daniel grimaced. "It doesn't look like the soul of a human being."

"*HE* will clean up nicely, don't worry about that," Kev retorted. "What would you look like if you'd been where he has, for God knows how long?"

Daniel felt a bit embarrassed, but Kev had raised a very interesting point.

"Kev?" he asked. "Does God actually exist?"

Part 11

Daniel was going to church with Grandma Brenda. Very grudgingly, it has to be said.

"I didn't go to church when I was alive," he grumbled, "so why do I have to go now?"

"To please me," Brenda replied, pushing a pale pink straw hat, decorated with a darker pink satin ribbon, down over soft white curls.

"Now, where are my gloves?"

"So where *is* this church?" Daniel questioned. "And how long will the service be? I remember going to a christening or a wedding, or something like that when I was a kid, and it went on forever."

"Of course it didn't!" Brenda tutted. "It's the right time for you to go, and that's all there is to it. The church is just over the hill there, so let's get going."

The air was soft and warm, filled with birdsong and the hum of busy insect wings. Brenda looked pretty in a blue and white floral dress, pink hat, and white shoes and gloves. She seemed incredibly happy to be going to church... excited even... and Daniel almost had to trot to keep up with her.

"Bloomin' 'eck," he puffed, "are we in a hurry?"

"Stop grumbling young man, you're getting more like your grandad every day. Here we go... just up the hill..."

Daniel couldn't believe what he was seeing. 'Just over the hill' implied something small, a little building tucked away. There was no building... no church as such. What there was was an apparently endless ocean of souls... he couldn't even begin to guess how many... millions maybe... gathered together in the sunshine. Some were sitting on the grass, others on smooth, flat boulders, the elderly seated on small wooden benches. There was a gentle buzz of conversation, and a wonderfully uplifting sense of friendship and love. Daniel was blown away... speechless. He stared, with eyes as big as saucers, at the most amazing spectacle ever. Every skin colour, every creed, every age group, sharing the same space, mile after mile, in complete unity and harmony.

"*This* is church?" He finally found his voice. "So where's the altar? Where does the priest do his thing? How are we supposed to hear him... where are the screens and speakers?"

"Oh, you'll soon know all you need to know! Now, let's find somewhere to sit."

An elderly American Indian guy, seated on a worn but comfy looking bench, shuffled up and patted the space next to him. Brenda squeezed in next to him, smiling her gratitude, and Daniel noticed that a little spark flew between them.

"Gross," he muttered, "they're too bloody old for that kind of stuff."

The grass was emerald green, bouncy and warm. Cross-legged, he settled down, leaving some space between himself and those around him. He wasn't quite ready to join in yet. He noticed that a lull was falling over the vast crowd, and that people were starting to close their eyes. Some held their heads high, others dropped their chin onto their chest. He supposed he should follow suit, wondering what was going to happen next, but as his eyelids came down, the strangest thing happened. Everything around him, the people, the fields, the hills… everything… disappeared. The ground below him, even. He was floating, hovering, still cross-legged, yet feeling completely and utterly supported. And he wasn't alone. There was a presence, one he recognised, without being able to name or place. He wasn't afraid, either. In fact, he felt happier and safer than he ever had before. Given half a chance, he'd spend eternity just hanging out wherever it was he was hanging out.

"Oh, I'm sure you have much bigger plans than that!"

The voice, filled with laughter, big, deep, warm, and soft, reverberated around and through Daniel. He shuddered, but in a satisfying, pleasurable way. As if something he had wanted all of his life, without even knowing that he wanted it, was about to be given to him right *now*, this very second.

"Are you… erm… I mean… is it possible? Are you...?"

"God? Am I God, is that what you feel a bit silly asking, Daniel?" There was the teasing humour again.

"Well, yes, to be honest, it is. But I suppose you'd know that, if…"

"If I'm God. I guess you're right. I *would* know it, if that was indeed the case."

"So, you're not?"

Of course it wasn't God… why would God be talking to a teenage no-mark who couldn't even cross the road properly?

"Why wouldn't God want to talk to you? You seem to be a pretty smart and interesting soul, and you certainly have a way with words! Do you think God only wants to chat with kings and queens?"

"I suppose so, yes. I hadn't really thought about it, but it would make sense that God would be more interested in important people than ordinary ones."

"Every soul is important, Daniel. That's God's opinion, anyway."

"So, ARE you God or not?" Daniel felt relaxed enough to be able to push the 'voice' a little harder.

"It depends upon what you mean by God, I suppose."

Daniel sighed. If this *was* God, he was bloody annoying.

"You know... all-knowing, all-seeing. Making people fight with each other, choosing who lives and who dies... that kind of thing."

"So that's God, is it? That's how God thinks and behaves? He sounds like pretty nasty stuff!"

"Well, that's what people say about God. I don't know much about it myself, but there are always wars going on, and I have heard loads of people say 'if there was a God why would he let this happen?' or 'why did God take my loved one when there are bad people on the planet?' And God *does* seem to be boring. I mean, look at the bible, and church."

"Ahh, I see. On the subject of church, didn't I see you there today with your grandmother? I thought it looked pretty amazing, but I am sure you are right about it being boring!"

"I mean normal church! That wasn't like the churches I have been to, with miserable hymns and old people giving you dirty looks every time you move. What I liked about it today was that there were people from all over the world there. I didn't get to see how it worked though, because I must have fallen asleep... this *is* a dream, right? Maybe there were going to be loads of different priests or preachers or whatever, taking it in turns to talk. I'm glad I fell asleep now, come to think about it... that could have gone on forever!"

"So, there are different Gods for different people, in different parts of the world? I can see how that could cause problems. All of those Gods fighting with one another? Mayhem!"

"Well, Gods don't fight... it's people who do, because they think that *their* God is the best, and that what *they* believe is right. They argue because of what their God says they should and shouldn't do, and they kill people they say their God wants them to get rid of. I suppose, thinking about it, if there *is* a real God, he must have a split personality or be a massive liar, because he seems to tell different stuff to different people!"

Daniel was shocked to hear himself saying the things he was saying. He'd never thought about any of this before, at least not consciously. And he still didn't know who he was talking to. But then, dreams are usually mostly weird crap.

"So, which God do *you* believe in, Daniel?"

This could be a trick question, the boy figured. If this *was* the real God he was talking to, he'd have to come up with a good answer.

"Okay, if you *were* God, who'd you support... the reds or the blues?"

Once again, a wave of warm, delighted laughter rippled through and around Daniel, and he found himself grinning mischievously.

"Hmm, let me see now. Which would *you* support?"

"The reds, of course!" Daniel snorted.

"Then it's a no-brainer... the reds it is!"

Part 12

Daniel stirred, yawned, and rolled over. He thought he was lying in his bed, on the crumpled-up sheet with the coke stain. He imagined he heard the loo flush in the bathroom next door, and the sound of music coming from Jade's bedroom… and then something pushed hard against his leg.

"Well, how long was I gone?"

Confused, Daniel struggled to open his heavy eyes, feeling as if he was surfacing from a really deep sleep. Another insistent, irritating shove did the trick, and Grandad Bill loomed into view as Daniel finally shook himself into consciousness.

"Wakey-wakey, rise and shine. I asked you, how long have I been gone?"

Daniel sat up, shaking sand from his hair, wondering how the hell he had ended up back on the beach with no horizon. He had had a dream… a really weird dream… but he couldn't quite remember what it was about. He knew he'd thought he was alive again, and in his bed, but the dream was before that. And this was the first 'real' dream he'd had since he died. Being dead was like being in a dream state… but it was as if this had been a dream within a dream. Disoriented, he stared up at the older man, who had clearly been pushing the toe of his shoe into his leg.

"What am I doing here? And are you back now, or am I imagining this too?" he demanded.

Bill lowered himself onto the sand next to the tousled boy, chuckling to himself.

"Yes, I'm back. And it looks like my tenner's safe. I hear you went to church with your grandma?"

Daniel frowned, disoriented… but something was coming back to him. People, loads and loads of people. The red indian guy on the bench, Grandma Brenda's pink hat. Closing his eyes… and the voice.

"Yes! I remember now! I *did* go, but it wasn't a church. There were millions of people, all outside, just over the hill. You should have seen them! They closed their eyes, so I closed mine, but then I must have fallen asleep. I was talking to… well, I don't know who it was, but I think we were talking about… God?"

"That's what I heard," Bill said, scratching his chin. "News travels fast around here. So, what do you make of it all now?"

"I don't know… it feels real, but it doesn't make any sense!"

Grandad Bill grunted. "Sense, eh? Since when did anything have to make sense to you, the daft bugger who can't even make it across the road in one piece?"

"Thanks!" Daniel huffed sarcastically. "That's really helpful."

The older man softened, nudging the boy with his shoulder. "So, how did you get on with him upstairs, then?"

Daniel stared at his grandfather for a few seconds, trying to decide whether or not this was another piss-take, but Bill, straight-faced, met his gaze.

"You mean, I was actually talking to God? The real God? No way, that's stupid! It was just a voice… an ordinary voice… well, maybe not ordinary, but..."

"Why is it stupid? What did you think God would sound like? Did you expect lightning bolts and thunder, and the four horsemen of the apocalypse? You'd have piddled yourself, lad."

Grudgingly, Daniel admitted to himself that was probably true. "Okay, I get that. But it didn't feel like I was talking to God. It was more like one of those chats you have with an older relative you don't really know or see that often. It was okay though. He even said he supported the reds!"

"Ah, that's the thing with God, you see; he's a people person. He knows us all better than we know ourselves, knows what makes us tick, and he knows the best way to approach us. And that's the point of church here; it's a chance to catch up with God, in our own *individual* way."

The penny was dropping for Daniel. "So, all of those people were there to talk to God? All at the same time?"

"Yep, you've got it!" Grandad Bill laughed. "Hard to believe, but there it is."

Daniel poked little holes in the sand with his fingers, quietly pondering all he had just learned. However, he did have one question.

"So, God is definitely a man, then?"

"Well, God is who you recognise God to be, it seems. God wants us to be comfortable with him… or her, if that's what we prefer… and is willing to give us as much time as we need to develop our relationship with him… or her!"

Daniel, listening intently, suddenly thought about the dimension of lost souls, and shuddered. "What if a really bad person talks to God, a mass murderer, for example? How does God handle *them*?"

Grandad Bill was impressed with Daniel's questions, though he wasn't about to let on. Keep the lad on his toes, he thought. He was doing very well indeed, coming on in leaps and bounds. More so than he recognised, in fact, but there was still so much more for him to experience, to absorb and learn.

"As far as I can tell, God doesn't judge any of us. But when necessary, he asks some bloody challenging questions! Anyway, your grandma's waiting for us with a pot of tea and some nice hot toast and jam... you know how she likes to feed us up, and you know how she gets when the food's going cold!"

Part 13

Daniel felt different somehow. He was changing, and not in a bad way. He was now able to think without being heard by everyone within a hundred mile radius, unless he was consciously directing his thoughts their way. He'd gotten better at visiting his mum and his sister, and it was odd how quickly time seemed to pass in the world of the living. His mum was less broken-up by his death now, and laughed more often. He could still see and feel the sadness within her, and knew that it would never disappear completely, but at least she was making plans and looking forward to things again. There were grey strands in her hair, and little lines around the edges of her eyes, but as far as he was concerned she was still really pretty.

Jade was taller, a bit plumper, and was working at the hospital, making appointments and dealing with loads and loads of people. She still talked to him in her head, and still cried when on her own and looking at the photo album she'd made after he died. And, she had a boyfriend called Si. He seemed okay, played rugby, and worked as a builder.

Daniel was glad that things had settled down for them, and that they were getting on with life. It was the same for

him, too… he was getting on with his own existence, and was learning something new at every turn. And, he had a feeling he was about to learn something else, pretty soon, because Kev said he had something to show him. It'd better not be anywhere like the dimension of lost souls, otherwise Kev could think again.

They were standing in front of a tall, rust-coloured brick building. It was almost as wide as it was high, with rows of small, square windows, through which nothing at all could be seen. There was a single door, at ground level, on the right side of the building.

"So, what *is* this place?" Daniel queried. It didn't look or feel scary, which was a relief.

"Read the sign," Kev said, pointing to a narrow board above the door.

"It says 'Revisiting Centre'. What's that mean?" Daniel had absolutely no idea what to expect beyond the narrow, dark blue door.

"It means what it says: 'revisiting centre'. A centre for those who are revisiting!"

Kev pushed the door, and it opened slowly, heavily, making a soft swooshing sound. Glancing at Daniel, he placed a finger against his own lips, indicating that they should be quiet. Daniel followed him in, almost tiptoeing, and couldn't believe what he was seeing.

There were sleeping souls, row upon row of them, from the floor to what was probably the ceiling, except that it was so high it couldn't actually be seen. Dimly lit, the inside of the building was warm, yet airy and cool. At first, it seemed as if there was no sound at all, but then Daniel became aware of what could only be described as a soft sighing. He also noticed that there was movement… busy souls flitting amongst the sleeping rows, checking and monitoring.

"Wow, what *is* this place?"

"I'll explain later," Kev mouthed. "There's something I want to show you first."

Daniel felt Kev enter into his mind, indicating that he should just allow himself to be led. He trusted Kev, and he didn't feel that there was anything to fear here, in this sighing palace of sleep. They rose, passing peacefully unaware men, women and children, before moving along one particular row, coming to rest in front of a tiny elderly woman.

"I would like to introduce you to your niece," Kev whispered.

Daniel stared at the woman, and then at Kev, and decided that this must be the areshole's idea of a joke! He didn't have a niece, and even if he did, she wouldn't be a million years old. Even his grandma looked young, compared to this woman. Kev stifled a laugh, and pointed at her again, insistently.

Daniel leaned in, looking more closely at the elderly, lined face... and almost jumped as high as the ceiling that couldn't be seen. The deeply sleeping soul before him began to change, facial lines disappearing, skin regaining moisture and plumpness, youthfulness returning... and suddenly he saw his sister, saw her smile... and he caught a glimpse of his own eyes. He also saw something else that he didn't immediately recognise, something indefinable. And then it came to him; Si, Jade's boyfriend. He could see him in the changing face of this old-young woman-child. He turned to Kev, silently demanding an explanation, but the older boy led him away, and within less than the blink of an eye, they were through the swooshing blue door, and back outside the building.

Kev, grinning, waited for Daniel to 'get' it, for it to click with him. Daniel, frowning, waited for Kev to explain. In the end, Kev had to go first.

"Well, did you see her? Your niece, Danielle Simone Brookstone? You've got to admit, she looks a bit like Jade, though she has got her dad's nose, and *your* eyes, poor kid!"

"I saw an old woman whose face changed, and it was… kind of creepy, but amazing, too. And yes, I did see something that reminded me of Jade… and myself. But, how does that make her my niece?"

As far as Daniel was concerned, this was just another weird situation for him to deal with, and once again Kev was involved.

"Think about the sign above the door," Kev replied. "Revisiting Centre. What do you think is going on in there?"

"I don't know… revisiting, I suppose," Daniel muttered.

"Bingo! And where do you reckon they could be revisiting?"

Daniel struggled to make sense of what he had just seen and heard, but suddenly, it *did* click with him. "Are you talking about reincarnation? Are you telling me that they are revisiting earth… being born again?"

"Double bingo ! The soul who *was* that frail old lady was once your great great great grandmother, on your father's side. She has elected to revisit the physical world, amongst souls that share her ancestry, in a brand new body. Your sister is pregnant, right now, to a daughter... your niece!"

Daniel was blown away and incredibly emotional... he was going to be an uncle (he preferred not to focus on the fact that, technically, it would be to his great great great grandmother), and they were going to name her after him. Well, the female version of him, at least.

"Thought that'd shake you up!" Kev laughed, excitedly. "Great news, eh?"

"I can't believe it... Jade, pregnant, me being an uncle... my mum, becoming a grandma! She'll love that, she'll be over the moon! Do they know, yet? I mean, they must do, if they've already come up with a name."

"Nope, they don't know just yet, but it's only a matter of days. And actually, where the name is concerned, that's me jumping the gun. I did a bit of digging around to find out what they were going to decide upon," Kev winked conspiratorially. "I called in a favour."

To Daniel, this was probably the most amazing thing he'd experienced since bouncing his way out of his physical life. Previously, he'd thought reincarnation was something that had been made up for computer games, not real. He had a zillion questions…

"I know, I know," Kev interrupted his racing thoughts. "We'll get to it, but let's go somewhere else."

Part 14

Anne Jackson was sitting at the little kitchen table, lost in thought, cradling a coffee mug. A smile played around the edges of her mouth, as she replayed the dream.

She'd been sitting right here, in the same spot, facing the door to the front hall. Daniel was in the doorway, lounging against the frame, smiling at her. He was taller, a little broader, with soft, gingery stubble on his chin. He looked really happy, and she was so pleased to see him… it was as if he had never left, as if he had just arrived home from somewhere, hungry for his supper.

She'd remembered she had some news for him… big news! "Jade's pregnant! You're going to be an uncle!"

Daniel had nodded. "I know! And you're going to be a grandma. We'll have to get you a rocking chair and a shawl!"

"Cheeky bugger!" She'd laughed. "I might be old, but I'm not ready for that just yet!"

"Well grandma, I have a secret… I bet you'd love to know what it is!"

"A secret, eh? Well, I'm not worried… there's no way in the world you'll be able to keep it," she'd teased. "You could never keep anything quiet as a kid, always bursting to let it out!"

Daniel smiling, eyes shining, had moved towards her, bending so that his mouth was close to her ear. "It's a girl, and her name is Danielle Simone. Love you, Mum..."

When Anne awoke from the dream, the scent of her beloved son was on her pillow, as if he had been lying next to her. It had seemed so real… as if they were actually talking, sharing the good news. And he'd told her something, whispered it in her ear, just before she woke up… what *was* it? She could feel it, on the edge of her mind, but couldn't quite bring it to the fore. Never mind… seeing and talking to her son again was enough. Some would say that it had only been a dream, an unconscious yearning, but she knew otherwise. And, weeks later, when Jade excitedly announced that the hospital scan had revealed the baby to be a girl, and that she would be named Danielle Simone, Anne Jackson had the strangest, strongest sense of deja vu. As if, somehow, she already knew.

Scanna (otherwise known as Mark Christopher Scanlon) was getting married. He wished that his best mate could be there to be the best man. Sitting on the edge of his bed, shoulders slumped, elbows on his knees, he wiped away a secret tear, one of a thousand he'd shed when no-one was around. He talked to Daniel a lot, and even though a few years had passed since he'd died, Mark knew he'd miss his best friend forever. He'd made other friends, including Josh Walker, who was going to be alongside him at the altar, handing over the rings and making a probably ridiculously embarrassing speech, but still… he wished it was Daniel. "Miss you mate," he murmured.

"He's marrying Jeanie Pearson… I can't believe it!" News of Scanna's forthcoming marriage had reached Daniel.

"Why can't you believe it?" Grandma Brenda asked, rolling pastry for a rhubarb pie. "What's she like?"

Daniel thought for a moment or two. "Like a pretty little Rottweiler. Well, she was the last time I saw her, anyway. Nice to look at, but with a right attitude!"

Brenda tutted. "Well, she must have changed, or Mark wouldn't be marrying her. He always had common sense, and was always a polite boy. I'm sure they'll be very happy."

Grandad Bill, peeking out from behind his newspaper (checking the obituaries and the sports results), caught Daniel's eye, raising his eyebrows at his wife's comment. "She'll make his life a misery and he'll rue it till his dying day." He winked, and Daniel grinned.

Brenda, pursing her lips, sprinkled sugar over the pie and slid it into the oven. "*You'll* rue it when you don't get a piece of this pie, with the lovely juicy rhubarb you grew in your own garden," she sniffed. "I like a good wedding. I've got the perfect hat... sky blue, with peacock feathers... haven't had a chance to wear it yet."

"You'll have to lend it to me laddo here," Bill grunted. "Sounds just like his kind of thing."

They were sitting on the little bridge that crossed the river in Calder Wood, legs dangling above the water. They were ten years old and skinny, with tousled hair, and trousers dusty and stained from climbing trees. Daniel had picked up a stick and was breaking bits off, dropping them into the busy water below, and they watched each piece as it was swept along, bumping against rocks, before being carried out to sea.

"So, you're getting married then?" Daniel commented, throwing a knobbly piece of stick with a leaf growing out of it, leaning forward, following its descent.

"Yep. Next week. Are you coming?" Scanna picked at a scratch on his arm, flicking a bit of scab at his friend.

"Gross! I don't want your dirty germs all over me, dickhead! Yeah, 'course I'm coming. Signing your life away to Miss Rottweiler… wouldn't miss it for anything. I hope the cake isn't fruit, by the way. I hate that stuff."

The dream made Mark laugh and cheered him up, but it also left him feeling a bit melancholy. It was only a dream, but it was as if he'd gone back in time, and he missed the simplicity… the endless days of hanging out and getting into bother. He decided he'd pay a visit to Calder and sit on that old bridge again, after work today. And he'd make sure that there was a chocolate gateaux on the table next to the far-too-frigging expensive, pale blue iced fruit cake. Daniel wasn't the only one who hated it.

Part 15

"We never really leave, because we can't. We just don't remember that. We all have different degrees of spiritual amnesia. If we didn't, it couldn't work in the same way."

Kev was trying to explain what he understood about revisiting. "It's one of those things that some souls know more about than others, and the souls who have revisited loads of times probably understand it better than those who haven't."

Daniel didn't feel any the wiser. "So, when Danielle is born, does the old lady disappear?"

"That's the thing," Kev replied, staring out to sea. "She doesn't. She's still here, like I said. But she changes. You saw that soul as an elderly woman, one that had been your great great great grandmother, but in reality that was only one part of who it is, who it has become. It's not just a 'she' or a 'her'... it has also been a 'he' and a 'him'."

Daniel sighed, shaking his head. "I don't get it. So you're telling me that even though that old woman... that soul… is going to revisit life on earth, she… it… will still be there, in the revisiting centre, after being born?"

"Pretty much, yes. It's like sleeping and dreaming. Remember when you first died, and all of your experiences were like dreams? You'd feel as if you were falling asleep, and then you'd find yourself somewhere? Well, that's still happening, except that now you've remembered *how* to dream-travel. It's easier for you, you've gotten back into the swing of things in this weird and wonderful world of 'spirit'. Things happen faster here because everything is operating at a higher vibrational level."

"Bloody hell Kev, you sound like one of those hippies or gurus, or whatever they're called," Daniel snapped. "So am I actually floating around in that revisiting centre right now, and just dreaming that I'm sitting here with you, on this beach?"

"Yep, and so am I. So is every soul. But me and you aren't preparing to revisit, and we won't get to see ourselves, because we are *experiencing* ourselves. Dead straightforward, really."

"Straight forward? Are you bloody joking?" Daniel was just about to become argumentative with Kev, when he realised that he was indeed joking.

"Look, you aren't going to remember the whole process any time soon… there is loads *I* am still trying to piece together, and I will probably have to revisit a million more times before I even begin to get close to the 'truth'." Kev was being deadly serious now. "But, this is what I remember up to this point; every human being is a soul, and is a part of a much bigger picture. We are like little pieces of a creative force, and we have been given the capacity for free thinking, and free will, and free choice. The more we experience, the more the creative force develops and grows, because *it* is us, and *we* are it… are you with me?"

"Kind of, I suppose…"

"That's good, because I'm confusing myself with all of this. Anyway, we don't *leave* here… that would be like an astronaut cut adrift, floating off into space, beyond rescue. Our *connection* is here, whilst our awareness wanders off and has a whole host of experiences, with a whole host of other souls. We can share dream-travels, seeing the same stuff as other souls, but from a different perspective, with a different interpretation of reality. It's a cycle that will go on and on and on, I imagine."

Daniel had a question. "So, what about the crazies in the dimension of lost souls? Are they in the revisiting centre as well? And if they are, I hope they're nowhere near me!"

"Oh, they're there too," Kev said, grimly. "In a real deep and dark dream-state. Free thinking, will, and choice, remember? A soul can choose how it responds to the circumstances it gravitates towards, even if those circumstances are not the easiest or the nicest. And, before you ask, I don't remember why or how souls choose crap lives… or even *if* they choose them. I do know that every soul contributes in their own way, even if it is only to be such a pain in the arse that other souls have to figure out how to clean up the mess they make, and turn it into something better. That seems to be how life progresses, in the physical dimension. Things have to be really bad before they can be made great. I might be wrong, but that's how it seems to work."

They sat in silence for a while, lost in their own thoughts. They'd met up at the beach with no horizon, but as Daniel gazed out to sea, something was taking shape and form, far across the water.

"Kev, what's that, out there?" He asked, pointing. "It wasn't there before."

"It was always there, mate. You just couldn't see it until now. It's something to aspire to, *somewhere* to aspire to. It's where your own higher dreams can be explored. You'll find out, when the time is right."

Daniel became aware that there were other souls on the beach, chattering and laughing in little groups. He recognised Micci, the girl who'd arrived with the ones who had died in an explosion. He was pleased to see how happy she looked, still wearing shorts, her slim legs still tanned, sun-kissed highlights in her hair. She felt his attention and waved a greeting, before turning back to her companions, a short, stocky man, and a tall, elegant looking lady, seated in stripey deck-chairs. And he felt the presence of Emily, his sister, though he couldn't see her.

"Kev," he said, turning to his friend who was lying back in the sand, hands clasped behind his head, eyes closed.

"What?"

"How come you're so smart? You seem to know so much, way more than I do, and it isn't as if you died a hundred years before I did. Can you remember who else you have been? Maybe you were someone really intelligent… before you became an idiot again, that is."

"I was Gandi, if you must know, but don't tell anyone."

"Liar!" Daniel laughed, throwing a handful of sand at him, before leaping to his feet. "More like Gandalf…"

"Daniel… hey, wait for me!" Emily's voice, dancing on the breeze, distracted him from further insult. He watched as she bounded towards him, hair bouncing, arms swinging, and smiled. She was like a sweet-smelling puppy, always enthusiastic, always happy. "Isn't it great about Danielle? I can't wait for her birth-day, can you? And she's being named after *you*, you lucky thing. That means you'll always be bound together… oh, hi Kev!"

"Hi, gorgeous. So you're going to be an auntie? Congratulations!"

"Yep, ghostly Auntie Em!" She laughed. "But, in the meantime, isn't there somewhere you should be, Daniel?"

He stared at her for a second or two, baffled… and then he remembered. "The wedding! Is it that date and time already? Bloody hell, how come time passes so quickly in the land of the living? I'd better get going…"

"*We'd* better get going," Emily said, as she linked her arm through his. "It's time you took your little sister somewhere, and I do love a good wedding… especially the cake!"

Part 16

Jeanie Scanlon (nee Pearson), in four inch heels, just about reached her new husband's ear lobe, but she had the look of a woman of who could conquer the world.

"Look at her hair, it's gorgeous," Emily whispered, as if there was a danger of being heard. Jeanie's tumble of almost black hair cascaded to her tiny waist, expertly tweaked and curled. "She looks like a little doll, she's so petite. You wouldn't think she'd be able to produce twins, especially two strapping boys."

Daniel stared at his sister, suddenly distracted from the sight of a grinning, relieved Scanna, heading back down the aisle (although the nickname now seemed a bit inappropriate for a married man). "Twins? What do you mean? I didn't know she had kids! Where are they?"

"They're not born yet, you daft thing! They haven't even been conceived, not until January." Emily giggled. "She'll get her waistline back though, pretty quick. Even after the girl, she'll still have a nice figure. Some women are just a bit more stretchy than others."

Daniel was blown away. "How'd you know all of this? You didn't even know them. And, how can you see kids who haven't even been conceived yet?"

Emily rolled her eyes and shook her head. "Just because they haven't been conceived doesn't mean they don't exist! I know them... I know the souls who are going to be David Mark Scanlon, Richard John Scanlon, and Gemma Louise Scanlon. David's a big softie, Ritch is a bit of a handful, and Gemma is pretty, but more like her dad than her mum."

Daniel realised that there was a lot more to the childlike soul who would have been Emily Jackson than he understood. He felt ashamed that he had not taken the time to find out more about her. *Too caught up in your own stuff,* he berated himself.

"Emily, what *is* it that you do... or where is it that you go? I'm sorry I never asked. I should've, but I've been too busy thinking about myself."

Emily laughed, kindly. "Of course you have... you died suddenly, and very young! That takes some coming to terms with. I will tell you all about it, but there's a reception to attend first... I can't wait to see how they've laid everything out, and what the colour scheme is!"

"Not all souls are going to go as far as actually being born," Emily explained. "Sometimes they realise that the physical body is not forming in the way they need it to, and so they delay their journey into the world. Other times, they allow fear to prevent them from completing the process; being born is a major shock to the system, for the living *and* the deceased! Can you imagine, as a human being, remembering what it was like to be born? Who could live with *that* memory!"

Daniel had learned that his little sister worked and associated with souls whose journey into the physical world was interrupted, for whatever reason, in a kind of midway stage between the revisiting centre and birth itself. He realised that far from being a simple, child-soul, Emily was wise in a way he himself wasn't, and he began to see beyond the image she projected. This was an old, incredibly strong, kind and loving soul, with endless patience and humour.

"And, sometimes," she continued, "the soul chooses to become what could be called a sacrificial lamb. Take Horace, for instance; he elected to be conceived by Alison, knowing that the pregnancy would give her the biggest shock of her life, and cause her to get her act together. She was seeing a married man who was never going to leave his wife, she was living for the moment without giving a thought to where it would all lead, and being casual with contraception. *And* she was in her thirties, so not in a position to be wasting time heading in *completely* the opposite direction to her own hopes and dreams! Horace had been her brother in a past incarnation and wanted to help her. He allowed himself to be conceived, knowing he would never actually be born, to give her the jolt she needed to sort herself out properly. And it worked! Although it was messy for a while, with Alison believing that it was the end of the world after her boyfriend dumped her, *refusing* to acknowledge the pregnancy, she survived… and is now happily married with a daughter. Horace knew that she had a better potential future and he wanted to help her. And thank God she listened!"

"That's bloody amazing!" Daniel was fascinated, and so proud of Emily. If she'd have lived, she'd have been a hell of a sister… just like Jade. And he felt incredibly sad for his mother, who had lost not only himself, but also this beautiful soul, and the way life would have been with her in it. He felt sad for Jade, too, but then remembered Danielle Simone, and everything was okay again.

And then he remembered what Emily said, at the wedding. "So, how did you know about Scanna's kids then?"

"Oh, I went and had a nosey around the revisiting centre," she admitted sheepishly, "when I heard he was getting married. They know me there, so it wasn't too difficult. It's so exciting, looking into the placements! Of course, it's always better when you know a soul is going to a loving family, but that isn't always the case. We just have to try and prepare a soul for an experience that will, in the bigger picture, play a vital role in the evolution of the human race, even though it will be incredibly painful to live through."

She sounded and felt sad, and Daniel sent her a 'hug', the way Kev and Grandad Bill had done for him. "Thank you," she smiled, as she hugged him back. "You really are the best big brother in the whole wide world!"

Part 17

Gerald Jackson drank himself into a reasonably early grave and left the world at the age of 61, without having seen his children for... who knows how many years? The alcohol was a bit like the iceberg that sank the Titanic... it wasn't what *could* be seen that was most destructive, it was the huge mass below the surface that did the damage. And, so it was with Gerald. Guilt ate away at him, year in and year out, especially after the boy's death. The realisation that it was too late for change - too late to make amends - sealed the fate of a man who never managed to be the kind of husband and father he knew he should be. He punished himself in a way that no-one else could, and died as lonely and sad a soul as could possibly be.

When Daniel discovered that his father had transitioned and was in recovery, he was struck by a weird mix of emotions. One part of him desperately wanted to see the soul who had been the father he had missed and yearned for - the father he could barely remember, if truth be told... the father who existed largely in his imagination. Another part of him wanted nothing to do with the aresehole who had walked out, leaving his wife without a penny, and two children to support. The arsehole who showed up every now and then, stinking of booze and making promises he never kept, before disappearing for good. His mum had done her best not to turn him and Jade against the useless loser, because she was a good woman… but they'd made their own minds up, and Gerry Jackson had ceased to exist for them.

"What're you going to do? Kev asked, when news of Gerald's passing reached him. "I know what a loser he was. My own dad was a bit of a wanker, but at least he stuck around. You don't *have* to connect with him, you know."

"I know, thanks Kev," Daniel sighed. "I think I'll speak to Grandad, see what he says. "It's funny, isn't it, all those years I wanted to see him, and I had to wait until we both died!"

"Yep, hilarious," Kev responded, dryly.

"There's always more than one side to a story," Grandad Bill commented, as he dug away at a patch of earth, turning it over and over, picking out little weeds and stones. "There was a time when your mum and dad were happy.

Only a short period of time, I'll grant, and a long time ago, but they set off with good intentions."

"So, what changed?" Daniel demanded. "As far as I can see, Mum didn't do anything wrong. It was him who left… he chose the booze over us, and he never even visited Jade when she was rushed into hospital with appendicitis. I hated him!"

"I know, son. And you had every right. But, sometimes people just don't have what it takes. They don't have it in them to do what needs to be done. And in the end they hurt themselves more than they hurt anyone else, even though that's not how it appears. Gerry, your dad, was the biggest loser of all. He didn't get to see you grow up, didn't get to share time with you, doing stuff like going to the match or swimming. Didn't get to see you and your sister opening your Christmas and birthday presents. I know it was his choice, but sometimes a soul doesn't know how to come home, once he's left. I am not condoning his behaviour, I'm just saying… "

"So, what should I do? Stay away from him and hope he rots… or go and see him? I'll probably punch him, if I do see him. What'd happen if I did? Would I end up in the dimension of lost souls?"

The old man chuckled, and threw a small stone at his grandson. "Stupid bugger, what's this thing you've got about the lost souls? It's not a place you get *sent* to, like prison… it's a place you transition to, until you decide otherwise. I thought all of that had been explained to you. You won't thump him, it's not within you. I can't tell you what to do on this one, son. You'll figure it out."

Part 18

The soul that was Gerald Jackson looked withered and pathetic. Daniel was shocked. It wasn't what he was expecting. In his mind, he'd envisioned a broad, intimidating, red-faced bloke full of shit. This was not *that* Gerald Jackson. This was an underweight, balding, shamefaced old man. Daniel could no more punch him than he could a puppy or a baby. He slumped, adrenalin oozing out of him like air from an over-inflated balloon. He didn't know what to say, so he said nothing. Calling this *thing* Dad was just not possible right now.

"Hello Daniel. It's really good to see you. I missed you son. I'm sorry I wasn't there when you…"

"When I died? S'no biggie. I didn't *need* you to be there. You didn't need me to be there when *you* died, did you?"

Gerald Jackson hung his head and cried. Real sobs, pouring from his very core, agonised, self-disgusted tears of genuine regret. Despite himself, Daniel wanted to reach out and comfort the broken soul before him, as if he was the parent and Gerald the child. He tried to send a hug, but was still too raw, and so he settled for a touch on the shoulder. "It's okay, don't get upset," he muttered.

"I know I let you down… all of you… you, Jade, *and* your mum. I was a mess. I had no right getting married and fathering kids. I should have done the right thing and let Anne - your mum - meet someone decent, someone who would have been a proper father to you."

Daniel, suddenly feeling a bit better, laughed. "Well that's a bloody stupid thing to say! If you hadn't married Mum, I wouldn't have been born in the first place would I? If she'd met someone else and had a son, it wouldn't be *me*, would it?"

Gerald wiped his eyes and sniffed. "I suppose not. You've got a point there. See, you're a smart lad, much smarter than I am. Thank you for coming to see me, it's more than I deserve."

"Yes, it is," Daniel replied, "but what's done is done. It's all in the past now. You need time to recover and think through everything, and then you can start again… work on becoming the soul you always wanted to be. It's not too late."

And, just for a second, Daniel felt a warm wave of Grandad approval flowing through and around him, and smiled to himself: "he *is* still listening in - I don't care *what* he says!"

Part 19

Emily was right about the twin boys, conceived at the end of January, due the following November - winter babies. And Danielle Simone was born a healthy 8lbs 2oz, with Daniel's eyes, her mother's mouth (and not just the shape, either, Daniel grinned to himself. At last, Jade would find out what it was like to be on the receiving end of her own tongue!) and her dad's nose.

All seemed well, until Anne became seriously ill. She had been feeling poorly for weeks, and both Daniel and Emily had been trying to get through to her, to push her in the direction of the doctor's surgery, but, stubborn as ever, she was determined to 'work through it'. Until that is, she collapsed at work, and stopped breathing.

"You stupid woman!" Daniel yelled, beside himself with frustration and fear. It wasn't her time, it wasn't supposed to be this way. Why did she always have to be the one to keep going, worrying herself sick about everyone else, whilst neglecting her own needs?

"She gets it from your grandma," Bill told him. "She hasn't transitioned fully yet, she's still in the process, so keep your hat on and hold your horses."

Daniel scowled, wondering whether there was a book somewhere, containing all of his granddad's sayings. "So, what's going to happen next? Will she show up here?" He remembered Lily, the girl who screamed for her mother, and he shuddered. He didn't ever want his mum to be that afraid.

"Maybe... just for a second... oh, here she comes..."

And there she was, his beloved mum, looking exhausted and bewildered, her hair a sweaty, tangled mess. She'll hate that, Daniel thought.

"Mum, it isn't your time, you have to go back! We tried to tell you, but you couldn't hear us..."

Anne Jackson thought she was having another dream, but this one was even more real than the others... she could almost believe that she was here, with Daniel... and Emily... and her dad and mum... she could see, hear and feel them all!

"Have I died? Is this it? I don't want to go back, Daniel... I want to stay here with you all! This is wonderful..."

"You can't, Mum!" Emily spoke up, firmly but tenderly. "Jade needs you, and so does Danielle. And you're going to get married next year, whether you know it or not! There's still so much more for you to do. And Jade's going to have a little boy… you don't want to miss all of that!"

Daniel watched as his mother, open-mouthed and wide-eyed, started to fade, to disappear from view, and he knew that she was reconnecting with her body. He was heartbroken and elated, all at the same time. He wanted to keep her here, to show her all that he had learned (or remembered, as Kev put it), but he knew that she had the right to live her life out, to experience everything available to her.

"There you go," said Bill, softly. "I told you there was nothing to worry about."

Part 20

Daniel had been doing some thinking. He had an idea, but it was massive… scary, even, and he needed to talk to someone else about it. When he thought about his plan, he felt incredibly excited, but also really sad. Maybe he was just being daft. Maybe it was seeing his mum here, when she had her near death experience. All he knew was that once the idea caught hold, he couldn't let it drop.

He decided to talk to everyone about it. He was really nervous, expecting a bollocking from his granddad, and mockery from Kev. He didn't care, he needed to get it off his chest, and so he'd face whatever was coming.

"I've decided I want to revisit," he announced, "and I want to go as Jade's baby."

There was a stunned silence for a second or two, before Bill cleared his throat and nodded. "I reckoned this would be on the cards," he said. "Especially after your mother's visit. Have you really thought it through… you'll be giving up so much here, you know."

"I haven't thought about anything else since the idea came to me," he almost sobbed. He hadn't even made his mind up to go yet, but already he was missing these souls with every ounce of his being.

"I think you're very brave, and although I don't want to lose you again, I will be proud of you forever," Emily cried, hugging him tightly. "And it is *really* exciting...a whole new life to create and experience, and at least you'll know your parents and your grandmother!"

"I don't think he should go!" Grandma Brenda huffed. "Talk sense to him Bill!"

"It's not up to me, Brenda, and you know that! The lad's got free will, and he has to make his own choices. 'Course we'll miss him, but it isn't as if we won't see him again..."

"Yes, but not as Daniel! He'll be someone else, not this boy here..."

Daniel hadn't thought of that. Spiritual amnesia, Kev said. But surely he would *still* be Daniel...or at least Daniel would be a part of who he becomes?

Daniel turned to his friend, the one who had been there from the start. "So - what do you think, Kev? Am I being crazy? What would you do, if you were me?"

"If I were you I'd definitely revisit… anything to escape being an idiot! I'd take the first body that was coming up for rent!"

"Thanks Kev, I knew I could rely on you… for *nothing*!"

They laughed, understanding one another completely. And Daniel knew, in Kev's own way, he was telling him he should follow his calling. He knew Kev would really miss him, but he also knew he'd be there for him, always within reach, forever and ever. They all would.

Part 21

"**A**lex Robert will be born on the 23rd of August, which means you will have to book into the revisiting centre very soon. You have to be there before the conception," Emily explained to Daniel.

"How much time do I have, then?" He was still nervous, still sad, and yet completely sure he was doing the right thing.

"Long enough to have a party, and say goodbye to everyone," she sighed. "They're organising it on the beach. Grandma's busying herself, still worrying about you going, and Grandad is still telling her to let it go!"

"I wish I didn't have to say goodbye," Daniel whispered. "I wish I could just go… goodbye is too bloody hard."

"Coward!" Emily teased. "It'll be fine, I promise. Come on, no tears, just laughter and love and togetherness! Everyone's going to be there, including Micci. I think she likes you, if you know what I mean!"

"Do you?" Daniel was surprised. "Bit late to tell me now!"

"He's doing fine," Emily whispered, as she and Kev looked over Daniel's sleeping form. He was smiling, as if he was in the middle of a really nice dream.

"He looks so young," Kev murmured. "I hope he has a safe birth and a good life. And I hope he makes it to old age this time, stupid sod!"

"I reckon he will," Emily said, as she leaned over and tenderly kissed her nephew's forehead. "Love you, Alex Robert; see you again one day. Give our love to everyone… and tell them we're only ever a whisper away."

Leanne Halyburton

spiritoflife@hotmail.co.uk

Other books by the author:

Our Life Beyond Death - An Incredible Journey

You Wear It Well - a biker rom-com

Printed in Great Britain
by Amazon

60932397R00068